To: Ivis

Happy Baking!
-Alyssa

To Mom and Dad,

Thank you for always encouraging me to dream big.

To my incredible grandparents. Thank you for
inspiring my passion for food.

-Alyssa

www.mascotbooks.com

Mimi's Adventures in Baking: Chocolate Chip Cookies

For more information, please contact:
Mascot Books
560 Herndon Parkway #120
Herndon, VA 20170
info@mascotbooks.com

Library of Congress Control Number: 2014921772

CPSIA Code: PRT0215A
ISBN-13: 978-1-62086-988-8

Printed in the United States

Mimi's Adventures

in Baking Chocolate Chip Cookies

written by
Alyssa Gangeri

illustrated by
Chiara Civati

Mimi dreamed of fluffy clouds of flour floating over mountains of chocolate chips with untouched ski slopes of sugar…

When she woke up, Mimi knew exactly what she wanted to do!

"Nonni, can we please bake chocolate chip cookies?
I've been dreaming about the ingredients all night!"

Nonni pulled out her giant cookbook
and they searched for the recipe.

First they collected the ingredients.

"Flour," said Nonni.

"Got it!" said Mimi.

Nonni continued, "Granulated sugar, brown sugar, butter, baking soda, salt, vanilla extract, chocolate chips…and lastly, eggs!"

"I got them all, Nonni!" said Mimi.

"Perfect! Now the equipment," said Nonni. "Cookie sheet…"

"CHECK!"

"Cookie scoop…"

"CHECK!"

"Parchment paper, mixer, cup measures, teaspoons and tablespoons, bowls…"

"Check, check, and check, Nonni! Everything we need is here!" said Mimi.

"Remember, Mimi…" started Nonni.

"I know, Nonni! Ovens are hot, mixers are stronger than me, and knives can cut me," said Mimi.

"And…?" asked Nonni.

"And I should always ask for help!" said Mimi proudly.

"Very good! We should start by washing our hands," said Nonni.

"Let's start baking! Our recipe tells us to pre-heat the oven to 325°. It will need plenty of time to warm up!" said Nonni.

"Now we need two sticks of butter, at room temperature. That's so it mixes easily with the sugar. Let's put the butter in this bowl to soften while we measure the rest of our ingredients."

"Check out my cool cup measures, Nonni! They all fit into each other! One cup, half cup, quarter cup, and a third cup," said Mimi.

"They're like a family of cups from biggest to smallest!" said Nonni. "Let's start with 1 ½ cups of chocolate chips."

Mimi measured 1 cup of chocolate chips and poured them in a bowl. Then she measured a ½ cup.

"Now we need ¾ cup of granulated sugar," said Nonni.

"Three of these?" asked Mimi with a ¼ cup measure in hand.

"Yes, three of those

Mimi scooped the ¼ cup three times to make ¾ of a cup of sugar. She made sure the measures were full to the top, and poured the sugar into a small bowl.

She did the same for the brown sugar, but instead she packed down each ¼ cup so it was nice and firm, like making a sand castle!

"Next is 2 ½ cups of flour," said Nonni. "I'll show you a trick my grandmother taught me when I was your age. Scoop a nice full cup of flour, then take a spatula and sweep across the top like a snow shovel, so all the extra flour falls off. Voila! A perfectly filled cup of flour."

Nonni read the next ingredients: 1 teaspoon of baking soda, ¼ teaspoon salt.

"Yuck! Why would we put salt into cookies?"

"I know it seems strange, but that little bit of salt makes the sweet a little sweeter! And, it helps the baking soda puff up your cookies!" said Nonni.

Mimi fanned out the rainbow of teaspoons and tablespoons looking for the right one. Just as she did with the flour, Mimi scooped, swept, and poured the measured amount into a small bowl.

"Now it's time for the wet ingredients. Use the red spoon to measure 1 teaspoon of vanilla extract," said Nonni.

Carefully, Mimi poured the vanilla extract into the teaspoon measure, and without spilling, poured it into a bowl.

"Well done!" said Nonni. "I hear you're very good at cracking eggs as well. We need two!"

Mimi smiled and took an egg.

"Knock, knock," she said as she tapped it sharply on the side of a bowl.

"Who's there?" asked Nonni.

"A crack!" said Mimi.

"A crack who?"

"A cracked egg, that's who!"

Mimi held the egg firmly with both hands, and placed her thumbs in the crack. Gently, she pulled her thumbs apart to separate the shell, and the whole egg slipped out!

"Ooooooo…egg-citing!" said Nonni.

"It's time to start mixing!" exclaimed Nonni.

Mimi sang, "It's mixing time…it's mixing time…"
Mimi began twirling around the kitchen and Nonni
joined in, doing the mixing time dance.

Mimi poured both sugars into the mixing bowl. With a spatula she slid the soft butter into the bowl, making sure nothing was left behind. They watched until the mixture looked like smooth, wet sand.

"Now we are going to mix until the eggs are broken up, but not completely mixed in. We don't want to over mix, or our cookies will be tough!" said Nonni, stopping the mixer.

"It's time to add the dry ingredients."

Mimi poured the baking soda and salt into the mixing bowl and carefully added the flour.

"It's a flour cloud, Nonni!
Like in my dream!" said Mimi.

"You've saved the best for last!" said Nonni.

They snuck a couple chocolate chips before adding them to the bowl. Nonni turned the mixer on one last time, and the individual ingredients mixed together to make chocolate chip cookie dough.

"Hooray!" exclaimed Mimi.

Nonni tore a piece of parchment paper off the roll and laid it on top of the cookie sheet.

"Is that so the cookies don't stick?" asked Mimi.

"Yes. I used to have to grease and flour the sheet when I was a little girl. This is much easier. Alright, time to start scooping!

"Make sure our cookies are four fingers apart so they have room to spread. As long as they are all the same size and have plenty of space, they will be perfect!" said Nonni.

Mimi scooped until the cookie sheet was full and the bowl empty. Well, not totally empty. There was still a little bit of dough clinging to the sides.

Mimi ran her finger around the bowl,
savoring every last drop.

"Mmmmm…delicious!"

"Our recipe says the cookies need to bake for
8-10 minutes. I am going to set the timer for
8 minutes, and then we'll check them."

"Are they done yet, Nonni?"

"No, not yet, but they're almost there!" she replied.

Mimi and Nonni set the table so they could enjoy the warm cookies with their family. Mimi skipped around the table, placing a small plate and napkin at every setting.

"Are they done yet?" Mimi asked again

Nonni shook her head and filled the glasses with milk.

BEEEEEP!

"I think they're ready, Nonni!
The timer is going off!"

Nonni checked the cookies. "Hmmm… they're not quite brown enough yet, let's give them another two minutes. Would you like to be my cookie guard, Mimi? You can use this button to turn on the light and check to make sure they become golden brown at the edges, but don't burn. Just to be safe, we will set the timer for another two minutes."

"Cookie guard reporting for duty!"

said Mimi, standing at attention.

Mimi carefully watched her cookies and
soon enough, she heard…

BEEEEEP!

"Nonni! They're done! The edges are golden brown!
Mmmm…the smell!" Mimi said loudly.

"They certainly are done! Stand back, Mimi."

Nonni put on her oven mitts, removed the perfectly baked cookies
from the oven, and placed them on a kitchen towel to cool.

Mimi didn't even have to tell her family the cookies were ready.
They were drawn by the delicious smell.

"Here's to Mimi and her very first batch of homemade cookies!" said Nonni.

"To Mimi, her marvelous munchies, and many more to come!" said Mimi's family.

Nonni's Chocolate Chip Cookies

2 ¼ Cups	All Purpose Flour
¾ Cup	Sugar
¾ Cup	Brown Sugar
1 Cup	Butter
1 Teaspoon	Baking Soda
¼ Teaspoon	Salt
1 Teaspoon	Vanilla Extract
1 ½ Cups	Chocolate Chips
2	Eggs

Makes 20 full-size cookies

Pre-heat the oven to 325˚. Place the soft butter and both sugars in a mixing bowl. Mix until smooth and creamy.

Add the eggs and vanilla extract until they are halfway incorporated into your butter mixture.

While the mixer is off, add the flour, salt, baking soda, and chocolate chips.

Place on low speed. Continue to mix until the dough comes together.

Prepare a cookie sheet with parchment paper. Place scoops of cookie dough two inches apart.

Bake in 325˚ oven for 8-10 minutes or until they begin to brown around the edges.

Allow the cookies to cool, and enjoy!

Feeling Creative?

Why not try some of my other variations on this recipe!

Replace your 1 ½ cups of chocolate chips with 1 ½ cups of your favorite nut. My favorite is walnuts!

To add a little crunch to your chocolate chip cookies, replace your 1 ½ cups of chocolate chips with 1 cup of nuts and 1 cup of chocolate chips. Best of both worlds!

Feeling healthy? Replace your 1 ½ cups of chocolate chips with 1 ½ cups of dried fruit such as chopped, dried apricots or dried cranberries.

How about we pretend we're on a tropical island and replace your 1 ½ cups of chocolate chips with 1 cup sweetened, shredded coconut and ¾ cup chopped macadamia nuts?

Sometimes I like to replace my chocolate chips with my favorite chocolate candies or chopped up candy bars!

Have fun trying these different variations or experimenting with your favorite ingredients!

Happy baking!

Love,
Mimi

ABOUT THE AUTHOR

Alyssa Gangeri is a pastry chef in New York City. She's loved baking from a young age. After graduating from The Culinary Institute of America, she traveled north and south working for companies such as the Ritz Carlton to gain knowledge and experience of the ever-growing hospitality industry. She has also competed on the Food Network's *Sweet Genius*.

She developed *Mimi's Adventures in Baking* as a new way of learning for the younger generation of bakers. Her love for baking shines through in this storybook cookbook. In her eyes, baking should be a fun experience adults and children can share together. What better way to do that then with an interactive story that makes learning your way around the kitchen exciting and easy!

When she is not making specialty cakes and pastries for her business AllyCakesNYC, you can find her in Central Park with her lively Jack Russell Terrier Rudy, and the love of her life Jonathan.

Mimi's Adventures in Baking Chocolate Chip Cookies is the first book in the series. Look for *Mimi's Adventures in Baking an Allergy Friendly Treat* coming soon!